Bella Donna

Ruth Symes thinks the next best thing to being magic is writing stories about magic. She lives in Bedfordshire and when she isn't writing she can be found by the river walking her dogs, Traffy and Bella (who are often in the river).

Find out more at: www.ruthsymes.com

Marion Lindsay has always loved stories and pictures, so it made perfect sense when she decided to become a children's book illustrator, and she won the Egmont Best New Talent Award. She lives and works in Cambridge, and in her spare time paints glass and makes jewellery.

Find out more at: www.marionlindsay.co.uk

Ruth Symes

Bella Donna

Cat Magic

Illustrated by Marion Lindsay

Piccadilly Press • London

First published in Great Britain in 2012
by Piccadilly Press Ltd,
5 Castle Road, London NW1 8PR
www.piccadillypress.co.uk

A catalogue record for this book is available
from the British Library

ISBN: 978 1 84812 249 9

1 3 5 7 9 10 8 6 4 2

Printed and bound by CPI Group (UK) Ltd, Croydon, CR0 4YY
Cover design by Simon Davis
Cover illustration by Marion Lindsay

For Hannah, Dona, Di, Ruby
and one inspiring 'holiday' cat xxx
R.S.

For Algernon, Grace, Sophie, Daisy, Tatty, Solomon
and all the other wonderful cats who
have ever crossed my path.
M.L.

Chapter 1

I'd never had a cat before I was adopted by Lilith and came to live in Coven Road. We weren't allowed any animals in Templeton Children's Home anyway. But now I have five cats. Mystica, Amelka, Brimalkin and Bazeeta are all regal

Siamese cats and their favourite place to sleep is on the bookshelves. And then there's Pegatha, a tabby cat, whose favourite place to sleep is on my bed!

I used to think all witches had black cats, but I was wrong. True witches' cats have become increasingly rare and most witches don't have one, however much they might want one. Lilith told me that most witches have never even seen a true witch's cat although she thinks she saw one once, a long time ago.

There aren't any in Coven Road even though everyone who lives in Coven Road, including Lilith, is a witch. Lilith realised I was a witch – or witchling as young witches are called – as soon as she met me at the children's home, even though I didn't know myself. She brought me back to live here, and I've never been happier.

Even though there are no true witches' cats here, there are lots of ordinary ones. Witches all like cats very much, but we also like other animals too. Our next-door neighbours have a dog called Waggy, and another of our neighbours, called Kelda, has snakes and alligators for pets. There are even unicorns and miniature elephants in the garden at the centre of our street!

Because Pegatha sleeps on my bed, she often wakes me up in the mornings by purring at me. But one Saturday morning she didn't make a sound and I woke up to find her staring at me with her green eyes.

'Morning, Pegatha,' I said, and Pegatha blinked as if she were coming out of a trance. 'Would you like some fish for breakfast?' I gave her a stroke – her fur is lovely and soft. Fish is Pegatha's absolute favourite food. 'If you want breakfast, we must get up then.'

'Blueberry pancakes?' Lilith asked, as soon as I came into the kitchen, followed closely by Pegatha.

'Yum!' Blueberry pancakes are my favourite

breakfast food and we often have them on Saturday mornings as a treat.

Even though Lilith could cast a spell to make our breakfast appear magically on the table, she never does that. We don't use magic for everyday things or we'd forget how to live normally and become very lazy. Besides, Lilith's home-cooked food is so delicious I'm sure magic food couldn't taste any better.

I gave Pegatha a bowl of fish-flavoured cat food – she's only allowed real fish on extra special occasions – and then I ate three pancakes.

Mystica, Amelka, Brimalkin and Bazeeta had already had their breakfast and were back on the bookshelves. They usually spend all day there. They're not that friendly to Pegatha for some reason.

Saturdays are my favourite day of the week. It's not just because we have blueberry pancakes, or because it's the weekend, but because it's when I have my spell-casting lesson. I love learning new spells and I love my spell-casting teacher – who's also my mum, Lilith!

Witchlings are only allowed to learn one new spell a week, which is a shame. That's because magic can be very tricky and it's especially tricky when you're first learning it. Magic isn't like ordinary school subjects — if you get it wrong it can land you in all sorts of trouble, and I should know . . . Before Lilith taught me to control my magic, I used to accidentally cast spells without realising. Once I even gave someone I didn't like a warty nose!

Lilith makes sure I've learnt each new spell really well and that I can remember all the old ones before she moves on to the next new spell. Luckily I'm a very fast learner when it comes to spell-casting — it's the only subject I'm any good at. Maybe it's because I love casting spells so much that once I've been taught one I don't forget it.

Lilith's niece, Verity, usually comes along to

the spell-casting lessons. She's a witchling like me, only she's a couple of years older than I am, so she's been learning for longer. Verity was jealous of me when I first came to Coven Road, and she was very mean to me. We're friends now, though I'm still a bit wary of her.

As soon as Lilith starts getting the cauldron ready for our lesson, Pegatha is there, waiting for us to start. She always comes along to the spell-casting lessons and watches everything I do. She makes me laugh sometimes when she has her little head tilted to one side and seems to be taking everything in! Not that she can really understand, of course, it just seems like she can.

'What spell are we going to be learning today, Aunt Lilith?' Verity asked, as soon as she arrived.

'I'm going to teach you a spell that needs two witches for it to work,' Lilith said.

We'd never done a double-cast spell before. Spells often grow stronger the more witches there are casting them. For instance, once a month, at midnight, all the witches who live here cast a protection spell on Coven Road so that no one who isn't a witch can even see the entrance to our road and would walk right past without knowing it

was there — unless we wanted them to. That spell is really strong.

Verity and I looked at each other and grinned. If Lilith thought we were ready to do a double-cast, she must really think we were making good progress.

'This double-cast spell allows you to create an exact copy of something,' Lilith said, 'although it will only last for a very short time before the duplicate fades.'

'Two of me would be wonderful,' Verity said, 'but I don't know about two of Bella.'

I poked my tongue out at her. If anyone else had said that, I'd have known they were joking, but with Verity I'm never quite sure.

'Here are the ingredients. First you need to decide what order you should put them into the cauldron,' Lilith said. 'You both need to throw the ingredients into the cauldron and say the spell at exactly the same time and then point to whatever you'd like duplicated. I'd suggest you try a cushion first.'

'Let's start with the cinnamon and then the gold candle, blood leaf and thistle water,' Verity said.

'Don't spells usually work better if the blood leaf goes in first?' I said, thinking about the other spells we'd learnt before.

'Yes, Bella's absolutely right,' Lilith said. 'But well done, Verity, you put the other ingredients in the correct order.'

I could see Verity wasn't very pleased. She doesn't like me being better at spell-casting than her, and I don't blame her. I wouldn't like it if it was the other way round, but it is the *only* thing I am good at.

'OK, you count us in,' I said to Verity to try to make her feel better.

'One, two, three . . .'

We each picked up a little of the ingredients and threw them into the cauldron as we chanted the spell together.

The words we use in spells are very hard to pronounce and don't come from a language people ever use to speak to each other – it's only ever used for casting spells. It's impossible to write down, but it sounded a bit like, '*Seeeorindggoi saheesta stowolhi staoorizlo.*'

Verity and I chanted once and then twice more before we pointed to a gold cushion with brightly coloured embroidery and beads on it.

'It worked!' Verity squeaked a second later.

And she was right. The result had been almost instant and where there had been only one gold cushion, now there were two. Usually we have to practise spells quite a lot before we get them to work as well as that.

'Can we do it again?' I asked. 'Can we try it on something else now?'

But Lilith shook her head. She wanted us to revise a different spell. 'I'll just get my grimoire from upstairs,' she said. Lilith writes down all her spells in her grimoire, which is a special book that all adult witches have.

'I want to try and duplicate Pegatha,' Verity said, when Lilith had left the room.

'No!' I said.

Pegatha hissed at her.

'Calm down, I was only joking,' said Verity. 'Stupid cat!'

'She's not stupid,' I told her. 'Pegatha's very clever and she's my friend. She's more of a friend than . . .' My voice went quiet. 'More than who? More than me?' Verity looked like she was about to stamp her foot. 'I suppose you'd rather have a cat as your cousin.' 'She's not just any cat . . .' Pegatha rubbed herself against my leg and purred so I bent down to stroke her. Truthfully I did like Pegatha much more than Verity.

'I wish she was a proper witch's cat,' I said. 'I sometimes think she can understand me.'

'True witches' cats are always black – everyone knows that,' Verity replied. 'Or sometimes black with a white star on their foreheads, but never tabby cats, like Pegatha.'

Pegatha jumped up into my arms as Verity said this. I don't know why but I always know when she's going to do that. It's like we can read each other's minds.

I didn't say anything to Verity though – she would only have said something scornful.

Pegatha pushed her face into my neck and I could feel her little heart beating very fast.

'I'd much rather have Pegatha than some silly magical witch's cat anyway,' I said.

'Huh!' said Verity, and she rolled her eyes so I knew she didn't believe me. 'One day I'm going to have my own true witch's cat, you'll see, and it'll be beautiful and sleek – just like me!'

'And probably have claws filled with spite like you do too,' I shouted at her.

At that point Lilith came back in. 'Everything all right, girls?' she asked us.

'Fine,' we both said, glaring daggers at each other.

Chapter 2

Once Verity had gone home, I asked Lilith to tell me more about true witches' cats.

Lilith sipped her chamomile tea thoughtfully. 'No one knows how or why but the cat always chooses the witch rather than the witch choosing the cat,' she said.

'So where do true witches' cats come from?' I asked her.

'No one knows that either,' Lilith said.

'What do they look like?' I asked.

'They're all black mostly. The one I saw when I was a girl had startling turquoise eyes and when it looked at me, I felt like it could see right inside my head.'

I stroked Pegatha as she sat purring by me.

'They're supposed to be magical, of course, and I have heard there are some true witches' cats that can even talk,' Lilith said, with a smile. 'But I don't really know if that's true or just a rumour.'

'They can *talk!*' I said. Now I knew why witches' cats were special. I'd love to have a talking cat. 'If Pegatha could talk I'd stay up all night chatting to her.'

Pegatha purred louder, jumped onto my lap and turned around until she got herself comfortable and then she settled down. Pegatha didn't really need to talk because I could understand what she wanted most of the time anyway. But it would have been very nice if she could.

'So you never wanted a witch's cat of your own?' I asked Lilith.

'I would *love* one,' Lilith said, 'but, as I said, a

witch's cat must choose its witch. I can't magic one up or put a spell on one of our regular cats to turn them into a witch's cat. I love them anyway, just as they are!'

I loved our cats too, but most of all I loved Pegatha. I pressed my face to her soft fur.

At bedtime Pegatha curled up on my pillow, but she didn't go to sleep as usual. She rubbed her paws against her neck and made a funny sort of sound – one I'd never heard her make before.

'You OK, Pegatha?' I asked, as I stroked her.

I checked the inside of her mouth in case she'd got something stuck or had a sore tooth but I couldn't see anything unusual. As soon as I let her go, Pegatha made the funny sort of sound again but then she went to sleep and it wasn't long before I drifted off too. Spell-casting can be exhausting because you need to focus so intensely on it.

A few times during the night I woke up having dreamt Pegatha was sitting on the windowsill under my witch mobile staring out at the moon and the stars and making that strange sound – almost a cough, or maybe a

hiccup, followed by a splutter and a sneeze. But then when I checked, she was always on my bed.

The next day, Pegatha kept on making strange noises, but nothing seemed to be wrong with her and she ate up all her food and played with her toys as usual. Her favourite thing to play with is a feather pen that my friend Sam gave me.

I got Pegatha to dance by using the pen. I always turn my music up really loud and dance across my bedroom and Pegatha runs after me and twirls around my ankles purring. Then I say, 'Up! Up!' and wave the feathery pen in the air. Pegatha stretches up on her back legs and waves her paws to try and get it. It's so funny.

'What are you two doing?' Lilith asked, coming into my room.

'Dancing!' I said.

'Looks like fun,' Lilith said, and she joined in our dance too, mirroring the steps I did.

One of the things I really like about Lilith, as well her being a witch and knowing amazing spells of course, is that she hardly ever gets cross and she's almost always happy. She never thinks anything I do is silly or childish.

'We should be on *Hex-Factor*,' I laughed.

The Hex-Factor is a talent show on TV which is just for witches. It's one of my favourite programmes.

Downstairs the doorbell rang and Lilith went to answer it while I flopped down on my bed and Pegatha jumped on top of me. I gave her the pen to play with. It's not looking quite as feathery as it used to.

'It's Sam!' Lilith called up.

Sam is the only person at school who knows I'm a witch. Most non-witches can't even see the entrance to Coven Road, and if they are invited to visit by one of us, they only see it looking like a very ordinary road. But Sam has been my friend forever – we both lived at the Templeton Children's Home for years, and were both adopted around the same time almost a year ago. The witches all agreed that we could trust Sam, and so he's allowed to visit Coven Road when he wants, and he can see the true magical Coven Road.

Sam came into my room holding a plant cutting. It had pink and white flowers and the leaves looked a bit like stinging nettle leaves. 'I brought this for Pegatha,' he said. 'It's called catnip and Trevor said cats really like it.'

As soon as Sam put some of it next to Pegatha

she pounced on it and then she started rubbing her face on it. She wouldn't stop. Pegatha didn't just like the catnip, she totally loved it!

'Tracey said she heard big cats like it too,' Sam laughed.

I was very glad Pegatha was a small cat. I didn't think having a lion or tiger rolling around on my bed and rubbing its face on catnip would be a good idea. Especially if it fancied a snack of fresh witchling to go with a catnip salad!

Pegatha rolled onto her back with the catnip beneath her and rocked from side to side as happy as could be.

'Thanks for bringing it round,' I said.

'That's OK. I wanted to . . . to . . .' Sam started to say but then stopped. 'What's wrong?' I asked him. It wasn't hard to tell there was something on his mind.

'You'll just think I'm being an idiot,' Sam said quietly.

'No I won't.'

He swallowed hard. 'Trevor and Tracey are thinking of adopting someone else.'

'What? But . . . not . . . not instead of you?'

Trevor and Tracey couldn't do that. They just couldn't.

Sam and I had made a pact when we lived at Templeton Children's Home that we'd wait to be adopted by the perfect parents for us – we'd called them our Forever Family. I'd waited for Lilith and Sam had waited even longer for Tracey and Trevor. Tracey and Trevor run our local Woodland Wildlife Centre. Sam's totally crazy about animals and so are they. How could

it not be working out now? He'd been living with them for almost ten months and up until today he'd never seemed happier.

'Not instead of – as well as me,' Sam said.

'Oh . . . but that's good, isn't it?'

'Maybe,' Sam said, but he didn't sound very sure about it. 'Only . . .'

'Only what?'

'What if the new kid doesn't like me?' He bit his lower lip. 'Or what if Trevor and Tracey like him or her more than they like me?'

I tried to reassure him, but I'm not sure how well I managed. I knew what the real problem was. Sam and I had spent a long time waiting for the perfect parent – or parents in his case – to turn up. Now that I had found Lilith I didn't want to share her with anyone, and I knew Sam wasn't ready to share Trevor and Tracey with anyone either.

We went downstairs and Sam gave some catnip to Brimalkin, Mystica, Bazeeta and Amelka. They all rubbed their faces against it just like Pegatha had done.

'Can you stay for dinner, Sam?' Lilith said, coming out of the kitchen.

'We're having pumpkin risotto,' I told him. I love pumpkin risotto, which Lilith always serves in a real pumpkin!

Sam shook his head. 'I have to get back,' he said. 'I promised I wouldn't be long.'

Once Sam had left, I told Lilith why Sam hadn't seemed very happy.

'A new brother or sister. How exciting!' Lilith said.

'You're not thinking of adopting someone else too, are you?' I asked, worried.

'No.' Lilith smiled. 'One witchling daughter is more than enough for me, thank you very much!'

I couldn't help being very relieved.

Chapter 3

I really wish I could ride my broomstick to school and see everyone's mouths opening and closing like goldfish when they saw me. I'd laugh and laugh as they stared and pointed up at me flying through the sky and then I'd do a loop-the-loop right past the headmistress. But unfortunately I'm not allowed to ride my broomstick to school, so I ride my bike instead. It can be hard keeping my magic life a secret.

'Gemma came home from the hospital!' my friend Angela said, as soon as I came into class on Monday morning. 'She's sooooooo cute.'

Angela showed me a photo of her new baby

sister.
Gemma was
wearing a tiny
pink woollen
hat. Pink is
Angela's
favourite
colour.
'She's
sweet,'
I said.

'I made her that hat,' Angela said. 'For something so small, it took ages!'

I don't have any brothers or sisters myself, or at least I don't think I do. I was left in a blanket on the steps of Templeton Children's Home when I was a baby. There wasn't even a note saying what my name was. Nurse Harrigan – who's now Matron Harrigan – at the children's home called me Isabella but I prefer to be called Bella, or Bella Donna.

Angela showed the photo of Gemma to Rajni and Katie.

'She's perfect,' Rajni said.

'Yes, she is,' Angela agreed. 'Only she doesn't like sleeping much, or at least not when the rest of us want to go to sleep!'

'It's very noisy in here,' said our teacher, Mrs Pearce, as she came into the classroom. 'Can we have a bit of hush, please?'

Everyone went back to their places and quietened down. Angela put her phone away in her bag.

'Today we're going to begin working on a new project,' Mrs Pearce said. 'Who can tell me anything about Ancient Egypt and the Ancient Egyptians?'

Lots of people's hands went up, including mine, and everyone started talking at once:

'They built the pyramids . . .'

'They made mummies, miss . . .'

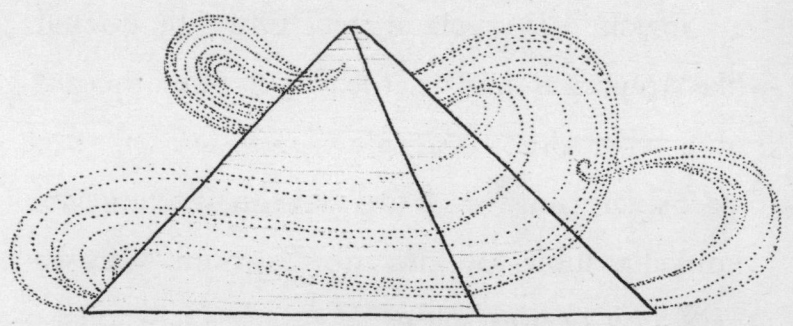

'There's a movie called *The Mummy*.'

'One at a time, please,' said Mrs Pearce.

Sam's hand was waving in the air like a flag.

Mrs Pearce pointed at him. 'Yes, Sam?'

'They had special beetles called scarab beetles,' he said.

'And do you know what else the scarab beetle is known as?' Mrs Pearce asked him.

'No.'

'The dung beetle,' said Mrs Pearce.

'Eeeow!' said most of the class.

'Wow!' said Sam.

'I thought you'd be interested in that particular fact, Sam,' Mrs Pearce said, and she smiled at him.

'Dung beetles are really clever. They roll up

animal dung into balls and then lay their eggs inside it,' Sam said.

Angela rolled her eyes and I grinned at her. Sometimes I can't believe how much Sam knows about animals. Or I suppose I should say insects, in this case!

'Very good, Sam,' said Mrs Pearce. 'The Ancient Egyptians believed the sun was rolled across the sky each day by a giant scarab.'

After break, Mrs Pearce showed us how to write our names in hieroglyphics. My name looked like a picture of a foot and leg up to just below the knee for the letter B, a feather for the E, two lions for the two Ls and an eagle for the A. Sam was really pleased because he had an owl in the hieroglyphics for his name.

'We've got some baby owls at the Wildlife

Centre,' Sam told me. 'They're called owlets  and they're sweet but are making the nest really cramped . . .' He stopped talking and just looked sad.

I knew he was thinking about what his home would be like with the new child.

'It'll be OK,' I said. 'Trevor and Tracey won't stop loving you just because they are adopting someone else too.'

Sam just shook his head. 'You don't know that,' he said.

And I didn't.

Mrs Pearce told us that the Ancient Egyptians worshipped lots of gods and goddesses and some of them looked really weird – they had the bodies of people but the heads of animals. The goddess Bast, or Bastet as she was also known, had a cat's head! I thought having a cat's ears and

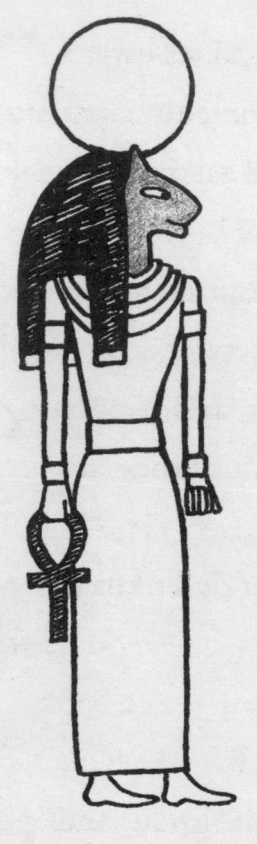

whiskers would be really pretty weird. Bast was supposed to be a gentle protective goddess but she could be fierce if she needed to be and then her head would change from being a cat to being a lion. Bast loved parties too, just like I do. And she played an ancient sort of tambourine called a sistrum.

'Have you got a cat, miss?' I asked Mrs Pearce.

'No, Bella, I haven't. Unfortunately I'm allergic to them. Cat fur makes me sneeze.'

'You could have a hairless cat, miss,' Sam said. But Mrs Pearce didn't want one of those.

'Did Ancient Egyptian cats look the same as

modern day cats?' Angela asked Mrs Pearce.

'Yes,' Mrs Pearce said. 'Ancient Egyptian people looked much the same as modern day people and so did their cats. Tabby cats are the direct descendants of Ancient Egyptian cats.'

'Really?' I said. 'I've got a tabby cat. Her name's Pegatha.' I didn't need to tell anyone that though, because I was always talking about Pegatha!

For homework we all had to do a project on Ancient Egypt. I decided I was going to do mine about Bast and her cats and I was going to take a photo of Pegatha to go with it.

'I'm going to write about babies in Ancient Egypt,' Angela said.

She'd already found out that Ancient Egyptian mums used to carry their babies everywhere with them in slings and the babies had rattles, just like babies do today.

Sam was going to write about scarab beetles, but he still didn't look very happy.

'Why don't you just ask Trevor and Tracey what's going on?' I asked him on our way home from school. Sam was walking, so I wheeled my bike alongside him.

'They don't know I overheard them talking about it,' he replied. 'I don't want them to think I was spying on them.'

We came to Sam's turning. 'See you tomorrow,' he said. Usually Sam walks really fast, or else he runs, because he's so excited to get back to Trevor and Tracey and the Woodland Wildlife Centre. But not that day. I was worried as I watched him trudge away, his shoulders drooping. I didn't like my friend to be sad.

I got on my bike and pedalled as quickly as I could to Coven Road.

Pegatha was waiting for me, just like she

always does. If it's sunny, she waits for me outside our front door. If it's raining, she sits on the windowsill indoors and peeps out through the glass, looking for me. But whatever the weather's like, she's always, always there. She's like a little cat shadow and my best cat friend.

I scooped Pegatha up in my arms and hugged her to me as her little nose nuzzled into my neck and she purred in greeting.

'Hello, Pegatha,' I said. 'Did you have a good day snoozing in the sun?'

Pegatha made a funny sort of raspy sound, a bit like the sounds she'd made over the weekend. It was almost like the strange non-words we use when we're spell-casting.

I carried Pegatha into our house. We live in a thatched cottage with roses around the door that are always changing colour by magic. There was a lovely smell coming from the kitchen.

'Had a good day at school?' Lilith asked me.

'Yes,' I said, and I told her about our new Ancient Egypt project while she finished making the tomato sauce for our pasta.

'Do you think there were witches in Ancient Egypt?' I asked Lilith.

'Oh yes,' she said. 'I know there were and they used to meet together in covens – just like we do today.'

It was amazing how similar things were thousands of years ago! Then I remembered what Mrs Pearce had said about tabby cats.

'Mrs Pearce said Ancient Egyptian cats

resembled modern tabby cats like Pegatha.'

Pegatha gave a little miaow at the sound of her name and that reminded me of something else. 'Did you know the Egyptian word for cat is *miw*?'

'I didn't,' Lilith said.

'And the Ancient Egyptians had pet dogs, with collars and everything,' I told Lilith. 'We know because a mummy of a pet dog was found in a royal tomb in the Valley of the Kings.'

'This certainly sounds like an interesting project,' Lilith said.

After dinner I worked on my school project about the Ancient Egyptian goddess Bast and her cats. Pegatha was very good and she stared straight at the camera as I took her picture. 'That's it, Pegatha – smile!'

Pegatha didn't smile but she looked very cute in her picture anyway. She might not be a true witch's cat but she was a descendant of the Ancient Egyptian cats and her little cat face stared back at me from the front page of my work.

'It's a shame you can't come to school and learn all about your ancestors,' I said to Pegatha as I stroked her. 'No one seems to think you can understand humans, but I bet you can!'

I put the work in my bag all ready to take with me to school the next morning.

When Pegatha and I went to bed, I dreamt I lived in a pyramid in Ancient Egypt with Pegatha and we didn't ride on broomsticks, we rode on a pet camel called Humphrey instead.

Chapter 4

When I woke up on Tuesday morning, Pegatha was still making strange noises, only now they didn't just sound like hiccups or coughs or sneezes, they sounded like something much more definite. Something that was almost clear and almost seemed to make sense, but didn't quite. The more I listened the more I was sure my ears couldn't be deceiving me – they just couldn't. Pegatha was trying to speak! The strange noises were Pegatha trying to say words!

'Lilith, Lilith!' I yelled. 'Lilith!'

Lilith came hurrying to my room. 'What's wrong?' she said.

'Pegatha's trying to talk!'

Most mothers would probably think you'd gone crazy if you told them your cat was trying to talk – but not a witch mother like Lilith.

Lilith listened carefully to the sounds Pegatha was making but then she frowned.

'Don't you think ... don't you think it sounds like she's trying to say "fish" or "wish"?' I said. The 'ish' bit was the most clear.

Lilith looked doubtful. I'd been so positive that Pegatha was trying to talk but as Lilith listened intently to the sounds she was making without coming to the same conclusion, I began to feel a lot less sure. Maybe I'd wanted Pegatha to speak so badly, like true witches' cats could, I'd convinced myself she was trying to do so when she wasn't really.

Lilith sighed as Pegatha kept 'talking'. 'Maybe she has a sore throat or is trying to cough up a

furball,' Lilith said. 'I'll give her some medicine.'

'You really don't think she's talking then?' I asked in a small voice.

Pegatha looked over at me and, if anything, the sounds she was making seemed to get even louder.

Lilith squeezed my hand. 'I know it would be lovely if she could talk,' she said, 'but honestly I don't think she can. Not really. Do you?'

I shook my head as Pegatha raced around the room like a little wild thing – she has moments like that. Now she ran across the floor and leapt on my bed and then leapt off it and raced across the floor again.

Lilith and I laughed as we watched Pegatha before she finally flopped down on the bed, exhausted.

'Time for breakfast and then off to school,' Lilith said.

Pegatha made the same funny sound again. I had thought it sounded a bit like fish. But perhaps it didn't really. Pegatha couldn't talk – it was just wishful thinking.

By the time I'd had my shower, Lilith had got breakfast ready and she'd also got some medicine to help Pegatha. 'Here, Pegatha,' she said. Pegatha didn't want to take the medicine at all and as soon as Lilith got close to her with it, Pegatha turned and raced out of the room.

'Oh, Pegatha, it's fish-flavoured and it will do you good,' Lilith called after her, but Pegatha didn't come back.

None of our other cats were making the strange sounds that Pegatha was. They were all sitting on the bookshelves as usual, watching us.

I had my breakfast and then called out, 'Pegatha!' I always gave her a stroke goodbye before I set off for school. But today Pegatha didn't come when I called her.

'I don't think she wants that medicine even if it is fish-flavoured,' Lilith said. 'I'll try her again later.'

'Yes — she's probably hiding,' I said, and picked up my bag. My bag seemed a lot heavier than usual. Normally I can swing it onto my back but that morning it was too heavy to swing. I decided I was going to give it a good sort out when I got home that afternoon — I had to rush to get to school on time.

As I cycled to school, I was looking forward to seeing what the rest of the class had done for their Ancient Egyptian homework. I hoped Sam didn't bring any real life manure from the Woodland Wildlife Centre to school with him to go with his dung beetle essay!

I put my bike in the bike rack with all the other bikes, although I'd much rather have been putting my broomstick in a broomstick rack. I was just taking my schoolbag out of the basket at the front of my bike when Rajni cycled over to join me.

Rajni's bike basket had a model of a pyramid in it.

'Wow! That looks really good,' I said.

'Thanks. It took ages to make and it was a bit fiddly,' she replied, as I helped her carry it into class.

She told me how she'd made it from cans and boxes from her dad's restaurant that she'd stuck together with glue.

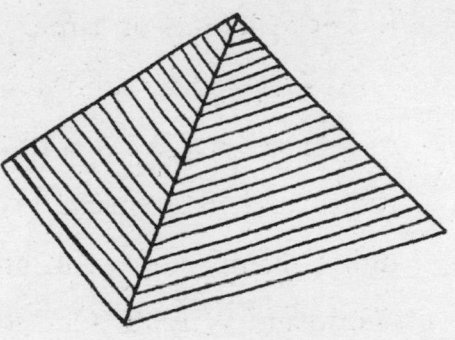

Angela was already in class when we arrived. 'Morning,' she said. 'Rajni, that looks amazing!'

I was starting to think maybe I should have made something to go with my homework too. Of course, if I'd been allowed to use magic outside Coven Road I could have cast a spell and conjured up a pyramid that would fill up the whole playground! But one of the rules is that we won't use magic outside Coven Road, except in extreme circumstances, and I didn't think homework would really count as extreme.

'How's Gemma?' I asked Angela.

'Sleeping a bit more, thank goodness!' Angela gave a sigh of relief.

Sam came into the class then. He looked even sadder than the day before.

While Angela and Rajni admired each other's projects – Angela had a doll dressed like an Ancient Egyptian in a sling – Sam and I talked.

'I heard Trevor on the phone last night. He said they'd be picking him up tomorrow. *Him* – so it's a boy.'

'Tomorrow? That's soon!'

Sam nodded miserably. 'And they were laughing and making *shh*ing sounds whenever they thought I might be listening.'

I shook my head. It was almost unbelievable. 'And they still haven't mentioned anything about the adoption to you?'

'Nope.'

It was really weird and not like Trevor and Tracey at all. They were usually quite thoughtful parents. Not telling someone that you were going to adopt someone else seemed really, really mean.

Mrs Pearce came in and we all went back to our places and sat down. 'Good . . . Atchoo . . .' Mrs Pearce said. 'I hope . . . Atchoo!' We all looked at each other. What was wrong with her? 'I'm sorry . . . I . . . Atchoo . . .' She fumbled about in her handbag, found a packet of pills and swallowed one. 'I'm very allergic to cats . . . Atchoo . . . Has anyone used cat fur for their homework?'

We all shook our heads. The closest I had to a cat with me was the photo of Pegatha I'd taken and I didn't think a cat photo would make Mrs Pearce sneeze.

'This anti-histamine should help,' Mrs Pearce said, and she did seem to be a lot better after she'd taken the pill. Or at least she stopped sneezing. 'Now we'll carry on with our Ancient Egyptian project. Does anyone know how they made mummies?'

None of us did so Mrs Pearce told us, although I wished she hadn't. They took the insides out and then wrapped the body up in cloth to preserve it.

'That's so yuck,' Angela said and I agreed with her.

'Did they unravel the intestines?' Sam asked Mrs Pearce. 'Intestines are ten times as long as the human body.'

I just shook my head. Some things you just don't need to know.

'I heard they pulled the brains out through the nostrils with a metal hook,' Carl said.

It was so gory. I felt a bit sick.

'After break we're going to be making something that I think you will all find very interesting,' said Mrs Pearce. 'Remember how we spoke about tabby cats from Ancient Egyptian times yesterday?' She pulled an object covered with a cloth from the second bag she had with her. 'Well, today we're going to be making our very own mummy cats.'

Mrs Pearce pulled the cloth off the object to reveal a papier mâché model of a mummified cat.

There were 'Ooohs' from most of the class and a yeowl of terror from close to my feet. It was a cat yeowl. Everyone looked round. I looked down. Pegatha's head was peeping out of the top of my bag! Pegatha was the reason my bag had been so heavy this morning! She must have been hiding inside it. She was also the reason Mrs Pearce had been sneezing!

Pegatha scrambled out of my bag and raced across the classroom, running in and out of the desk legs and jumping over people's bags. She managed to avoid every hand that tried to grab her.

'Pegatha, stop!' I cried, and I ran after her.

'What's a real cat doing in this – *Atchoo! Atchoo!* – classroom?' Mrs Pearce shouted, just as the headteacher opened the door.

'Hello, how are we —?'

'Nooooo!' I yelled, but it was too late - Pegatha had run past the headteacher and was now out in the corridor.

'Isabella!' the headteacher said crossly as I ran past her too. 'Isabella, come back here!'

But I didn't stop – I raced down the corridor after Pegatha.

I almost caught her at the end of the corridor but then someone opened the door that led to the gym. Pegatha ran under all the children clinging to climbing ropes and jumping over vaulting horses and I caused even more chaos as I ran after her.

'Oops . . . Sorry . . . 'Scuse me!'

I watched in horror as Pegatha, almost in slow motion, leapt up towards a high window that had been opened to let in some fresh air and jumped through it.

l couldn't even reach the window, and was far too big to follow her anyway, so I ran back through the gym, down the corridor, opened the doors and went outside into the playground. I still might have been able to catch her as she ran out of the playground and down the street, but the caretaker stopped me at the gates.

'Oh no you don't. Why aren't you in class?'

'My cat —'

The headteacher arrived then and even though I told them both about Pegatha they wouldn't let me go after her.

'I'm sure she'll be perfectly fine and you'll find her back at home, safe and sound, once school is over,' the headteacher said.

'But —'

'Back to your class - now.'

The day seemed to go on forever and I couldn't think about anything besides Pegatha.

What had she been doing in my bag?

'She probably has run home,' Angela said. 'Cats are very clever like that.'

But how would Pegatha know the way home from school when she'd been hidden in my bag and hadn't seen the way we'd come? I felt very worried indeed.

Angela lent me her phone so I could call Lilith but Lilith didn't answer and I didn't want to leave a message in case she got worried too.

As soon as the bell rang for the end of school, I grabbed my bike and rode like the wind all the way home.

'Please let Pegatha be there, please let Pegatha be there, please let Pegatha be there . . .' I wished, and I pedalled as fast as I could.

Chapter 5

Lilith was beside her cauldron working on a spell as I burst through the front door, gasping for breath.

'Bella?' she said in surprise.

Mystica, Brimalkin, Bazeeta and Amelka all

turned and stared at me from the bookshelf. It was as if they knew!

But there was no Pegatha to greet me.

'What is it? What's wrong?' Lilith called after me, as I raced up the stairs.

'Please let Pegatha be lying on my pillow, please let Pegatha be lying on my pillow . . .'

I threw open my bedroom door only to find my bed empty. No Pegatha. I felt sick and dizzy and sank down onto my bed as Lilith came into the room.

'Something terrible has happened,' I told her, and although I tried to stop them, hot tears streamed down my face.

'What's wrong? Are you hurt? Was someone mean to you?' Lilith asked. She sat down on the bed beside me. Her face looked so concerned.

I shook my head and sniffed noisily, although Lilith says it isn't polite to do that. 'It's Pegatha ...'

'What about Pegatha?'

'She came to school with me. I didn't know she was there, she must have ... have hidden in my bag and then Mrs Pearce ...' I trailed off as I suddenly thought of something. I had been about to say that Mrs Pearce had been talking about mummies, and that we were going to make cat mummies. And that's when Pegatha had screeched and leapt out of the bag ... Had Pegatha heard Mrs Pearce and got very scared? Had she thought we were going to turn *her* into a mummy?

'But what was she doing in your bag?' said Lilith, interrupting my thoughts.

'I don't know. I didn't put her in it. She must have climbed in or maybe she fell in . . .' And then I told Lilith exactly what had happened, and how I thought Pegatha might have understood Mrs Pearce and thought we were making real cat mummies!

Lilith hugged me to her. 'I'm sure she's probably somewhere nearby. I don't think Pegatha could really understand, do you? I expect she was scared to wake up in a strange place.'

We went outside and called Pegatha's name and looked all over Coven Road for her and asked every witch we met if they'd seen her but no one had.

If she'd fallen into my schoolbag by accident then why hadn't she made a sound? Pegatha is usually good at letting everyone know, very loudly, if there's something wrong. But that didn't matter now. All that mattered was that Pegatha was gone.

'What if she's lost and can't find her way home? Anything might have happened to her,' I said, with tears in my eyes.

'I know what we should do,' Lilith said, and we ran back to our house.

Lilith hurried up to her room and came back with her crystal ball and her grimoire. 'We'll see if we can find her with these.'

She gave me the crystal ball to hold while she turned the pages of the grimoire.

'Here it is.' She traced her finger over the spell that let her see images inside the crystal ball. 'Lavender,' she said. 'Get me some lavender from the garden – quick!'

I raced to get Lilith the ingredients she needed for the spell. 'White candle . . . gold resin . . . silverbirch-pepper . . .'

Once Lilith had all she required, she threw everything into the cauldron and began to chant: '*Hoooonyaza . . . hellingabaal . . . hallazareti . . .*'

The crystal ball, which only a moment before had been perfectly clear, began to form swirling shadowy shapes as Lilith chanted. We both leant forward to have a better look. Inside the ball the shadows seemed almost like clouds – ghostly shapes moving about – but I couldn't see a cat shape amongst them. Where was Pegatha? If only the crystal ball would show us.

Lilith circled her hands around the glass,

without ever touching it, and repeated the spell.

The ghost-like shapes within it moved again but there was still no Pegatha.

'Where is she?' I cried. 'You don't think she's – she's . . .' I couldn't say the word dead. But Lilith understood what I meant.

'You try the spell,' she said. 'There's always

been a special bond between the two of you. I think we can bend the rules about only learning one spell a week for this emergency.'

I wasn't feeling hopeful that it would work, as it hadn't done for Lilith, but I threw more ingredients into the cauldron and repeated the spell. '*Hoooonyaza . . . hellingabaal . . . hallazareti . . .*'

The ghostly shapes appeared again but still neither of us could see Pegatha or even a cat shape amongst them. I was so disappointed.

'Oh, Pegatha, where are you?' I said. 'Please come home.'

The ghostly shapes faded away. Lilith looked very worried. 'I don't know why we can't see her in this crystal ball . . . The only time it hasn't worked for me before is when someone had a hiding spell cast on them, and I don't see how that could have happened.'

I didn't see how it could have happened either. 'No one would do that,' I said. 'Everyone loves Pegatha.'

But then I remembered that not absolutely everyone did. Verity didn't and Pegatha certainly didn't love her either. Would Verity? Could Verity? Maybe. I wouldn't put anything past her. But Pegatha had disappeared from school and Verity didn't even go to my school. So she couldn't have done anything. She couldn't have. Or could she?

'I need to ask Zorelda,' said Lilith. 'She'll be able to help. Perhaps I'm doing something wrong.'

Zorelda was the Grand Sorceress of

Coven Road and if anyone was powerful enough to make a spell work, it would be her. She's also very wise, though I find her a little bit scary too.

'Let's ask her now,' I said.

'I wish we could but she's guest of honour at the Witches Convention in Witchwood this year and won't be back until Thursday,' Lilith said.

'So what are we going to do?'

'We'll have to try and find Pegatha without magic,' Lilith replied.

'Right.'

Lilith grabbed the phone and started ringing everyone she thought might be able to help us find Pegatha.

I switched on the computer and emailed everyone I knew and asked them to keep a look out for Pegatha and then I started making Missing Cat posters.

Missing Cat

Her name is Pegatha.
She is a tabby cat.
Her favourite food is fish.
Please help us find her
and bring her home.

No sooner had Lilith put the phone down than Sam rang.

'Did you find Pegatha?' he asked.

'No,' I said. 'I'm going to put up Missing Cat posters.'

'I'm on my way to help.'

Angela rang too. 'Did you contact Lost Cat?' she asked. 'Mum said the missing pet register are good. Can you email me a photo of Pegatha? I'll send it to everyone at school.'

'Yes,' I said, and I emailed Angela the photo I'd taken for our Ancient Egyptian homework.

The printer shot out fifty Missing Cat posters and as soon as Sam arrived we set off to put them up. Lilith stayed at home to phone every cat rescue home in the area.

Sam and I cycled round the streets, looking for Pegatha, putting up posters, and asking everyone we met if they'd seen a small tabby cat.

'She's very friendly,' I told people who were coming home from work, 'and she likes fish.'

But no one had seen her.

'She could be anywhere by now,' Sam said. Which I knew – but didn't like to think about.

We even cycled as far as Templeton Children's Home.

'Let's ask them if they've seen her,' Sam said, nodding at the door.

I knew that was very unlikely, but I felt a bit guilty for not having been back to visit the children's home in such a long time. I'd promised when I'd left and gone to live with Lilith that I would.

'OK,' I said.

We left our bikes by the side of the door and rang the doorbell.

'Sam! Bella!' Maisie said, as soon as she opened the door. Maisie had been our careworker. She had a huge grin on her face at the sight of us. 'How lovely to see you. Come in, come in. Matron will be so pleased to see you, too.'

'We're looking for my missing cat, Pegatha,' I said.

But Maisie wasn't really listening. 'This way,' she said, as she headed off towards the dining room. 'Not that I need to tell you two where anything is around here!'

She threw open the dining room door and shouted, 'Look who's here.'

Twenty pairs of eyes – from the youngest toddlers to Matron Harrigan – turned to look at us.

'Bella and Sam – how good to see you,' Matron Harrigan said, standing up and hurrying over to us.

They were having a birthday tea for one of the children and the five candles were already lit.

'One, two, three,' Matron Harrigan said, and everyone started to sing 'Happy Birthday' very loudly so no one could hear anything about us looking for Pegatha until the song was over and the candles had been blown out and the cheering and clapping was all done.

'So, to what do we owe the pleasure of your

visit?' Matron Harrigan asked us and I was finally able to tell her about Pegatha going missing.

'I'm sure she'll turn up,' Matron Harrigan said, although she couldn't really know that. 'My sister lost her cat. Poor Florence was so worried she couldn't eat or sleep, but her cat appeared three months later, perfectly healthy and looking well fed. The cat had been looked after by a woman two streets over who had no idea of the torment my poor sister had been going through.'

'My cat always comes running when I shake his box of biscuits,' Maisie said. 'Even from three gardens away.'

'Let us know when you find her,' Matron Harrigan said, as she saw us out.

'Come back and visit us again soon,' said Maisie. 'And bring Pegatha!'

'You know, I think it'll be OK,' Sam said, as we climbed back onto our bikes.

'What will?' I asked him.

'Having a brother. Everyone should have that chance to live with a family of their own. Just as long as the new boy likes animals as much as I do.'

I smiled at him, and we cycled on. Seeing everyone at the children's home had reminded me how we'd waited for so long because we wanted to be adopted by just the right people for us – and it had been worth the wait. I wanted other kids to be as happy as Sam and I were. Not that being at the children's home had been bad – it hadn't. I especially liked it when we had butterscotch tart for dessert and when we went to see *Wolves and Witches* at the cinema. But it wasn't as good as living with Lilith.

Half an hour later there was still no sign of Pegatha. I was seriously beginning to wonder if we would *ever* find her.

Sam looked at his watch. 'I'd better get back

or Trevor and Tracey will be freaking out and sending a search party to look for me,' he said.

I didn't want to give up looking for Pegatha until I'd found her, but I knew he was right. Lilith would be worrying too. 'I'd better get back as well,' I said.

By the time I got home, Lilith had phoned round all the cats' homes in case someone had found her and taken her there, and all the vets in case Pegatha had been injured.

'It's surprising how many places and people there are out there who want to help,' Lilith said. As well as the Missing Pet Register, she'd contacted Cat Chat, My Moggy, Pet Lovers Online and Lost My Cat.

They had all given advice and tried to reassure her that cats usually came home.

'They said putting up Missing Cat posters in your local area, like you've done, often has the best results,' she said.

But I was still worried Pegatha had been knocked over and was lying injured somewhere – or worse, but I refused to let myself think about that. She'd been in such a panic, she could easily have run out into the road without looking.

'None of the cats' homes have seen Pegatha, but they all took our number and said they'd call us if someone brought her in or they heard anything,' Lilith said, as she made me a sandwich.

'Try and eat something. Just one mouthful.'

I bit into the bread and rolled it around in my mouth but I couldn't swallow it because of the worry lump I had in my throat.

'How long have you had Pegatha?' I asked Lilith.

Apparently Pegatha had turned up at Lilith's house one day, a few weeks before I came to live here. Lilith had tried to find out who she belonged to but no one claimed her. 'So she's been living in Coven Road for nearly a year and has always seemed very happy,' Lilith said.

'Until I took her to school.'

I wished I'd checked my bag sooner, but I kept my pencils and pens in the side-pocket, and I hadn't opened the main part of my bag that whole morning. I'd thought it was very heavy. Why hadn't I realised Pegatha was hiding inside it?

'Don't blame yourself,' Lilith said. 'It really wasn't your fault.'

'But I can't help thinking that Pegatha was

frightened of the cat mummy!' I said. It *was* all
my fault. In fact, I think I told her she'd find the
lesson very interesting. I'd put the idea in her
mind.

Lilith squeezed my hand. 'I know Pegatha's a
very clever cat . . .'

I nodded as a tear slipped down my face.

'. . . but I'm sure she didn't know what the cat
mummy was. And she couldn't really have
understood what was said, could she?'

I shrugged. Secretly I thought Pegatha could.
She's *very* clever.

'As I said before, it was probably something
else that frightened her and made her run away,'
Lilith said. 'The sound of a scraping chair or
maybe you, or someone else, accidentally kicked
the bag she was hiding in. That sounds much
more likely, doesn't it?'

Lilith was right. It did sound more likely.

I went over to the computer. Lots of emails about Pegatha had arrived while I was away. One of them was from Verity.

Poor Pegatha :-(

I was really cross when I read it because I knew Verity didn't care at all about Pegatha.

You're such a fake! I typed back and pressed send.

If that's how you feel I won't help you look for her, Verity typed back.

Good. Don't want you to.

I won't!

I was so cross my fingers pressed extra hard on the keys. *Don't!* I typed. And then I switched off the computer before she could reply.

Lilith put a mug of hot chocolate in front of me. 'You look very cross,' she said.

'I am,' I said. 'Sometimes Verity drives me crazy.'

Chapter 6

I couldn't get to sleep without Pegatha there. I missed her little warm furry body and I missed her purring and the sounds she makes when she's asleep. There'd never been a single night since I'd come to Coven Road that Pegatha hadn't slept on my bed and my room was too quiet and lonely without her. Before I came to live here Lilith said Pegatha used to go to sleep in her cat basket.

I climbed out of bed and went over to the

window. Where was Pegatha? Was she outside somewhere, cold and frightened? Was she injured? Or had someone taken her in? And if they had, would they give her back? I knew if a cat like Pegatha turned up at my house one day I'd want to keep her and never let her go.

'Please come home, Pegatha,' I whispered.

I heard a sound coming from the kitchen and raced downstairs to see if it was Pegatha squeezing through the cat flap. But it wasn't Pegatha – it was Lilith.

'Can't sleep either?' she said when she saw me.

I shook my head. 'I'm so worried about Pegatha.'

Lilith squeezed my shoulder. 'Me too.'

The clock struck midnight. The witching hour. I looked over at my broomstick resting beside Lilith's. If only . . .

I looked at Lilith. She was looking at her broomstick as well!

'We might be able to spot her from our broomsticks,' she said. 'She might see us searching for her, too.'

'But what about the rules?'

All the witches of Coven Road have to promise not to use magic outside Coven Road except in very special circumstances, like an emergency.

'I think we can certainly say this is an emergency, don't you?' Lilith said.

I nodded.

'Wrap up warm. It can get cold at night riding on a broomstick.'

I pulled on my coat and gloves and a hat and

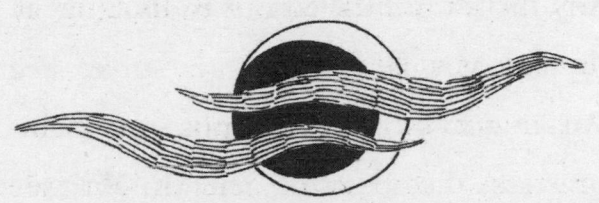

then I grabbed my broomstick and headed outside into the garden. I could feel the broomstick tingle as I held it and I knew it wanted to help me find Pegatha. She'd been the only other one to ride on it apart from me.

'Ready?' Lilith said.

'Ready.'

We climbed onto our broomsticks and flew up into the sky; far enough up to miss the trees but not so high that we wouldn't be able to see Pegatha on the ground, unless she was hiding.

I very surprised when we were joined by Mr and Mrs Robson – the witches from next door. News travels quickly in Coven Road.

'Any luck?' they called out to us.

Mr and Mrs Robson always stroke Pegatha and make a fuss of her. Pegatha and their dog, Waggy, are the best of friends. Waggy was helping in the search for Pegatha too - only he wasn't on a broomstick. He was running along on the ground, sniffing the ground and wagging his tail, looking up at us every now and again.

'Waggy's very good at finding things,' Mrs Robson said kindly as she flew past me.

But Waggy didn't seem to be having much luck finding Pegatha that night.

As we flew through the sky, more and more witches came out of Coven Road on their broomsticks to help us. Even Redbeard (who looks like a pirate and has a long red beard) came

on the search, although he didn't look very steady on his broomstick.

'Haven't ridden this thing in years,' he said, laughing, as he suddenly slipped upside down.

Soon it seemed like every witch from Coven Road was out looking for Pegatha but *still* none of us could see her.

As we flew near Angela's house, I saw that some of the lights were on, although all the other houses in her street were in darkness. I couldn't resist flying a little closer on my broomstick.

Then I heard a loud wailing – a very loud wailing! Gemma was keeping everyone up. Through a gap in the curtains I could see Angela's mum walking up and down patting Gemma on the back. I desperately wanted to tap on the window of Angela's room and give her a surprise! I knew I couldn't though – it was important that no one outside Coven Road knew we were witches.

Verity flew over to us on her broomstick. 'Any luck?' she asked.

I shook my head.

'Poor little cat,' Verity said.

I bit my bottom lip to try and stop myself but the words came out anyway. 'I bet you don't care if she never comes back!' I shouted at her.

Verity pulled a face and flew away and even though I knew I was being a bit mean, I didn't follow her or say sorry. After all, I couldn't be sure that Verity hadn't done something to stop me from finding Pegatha.

It was hard not to cry. I so wanted to find Pegatha, safe and sound. But where was she?

The clouds covered the moon and the stars and it started to rain.

'I think we should go home,' Lilith said.

I didn't want to, but I didn't know where else we could look.

All I could hope as we slowly flew home was that Pegatha was somewhere dry.

Chapter 7

'Time to get up, Bella,' Lilith called to me the
next morning, and I woke up from my dream
where Pegatha had been fast asleep beside me,
only to find she wasn't there.

It broke my heart to see Pegatha's empty bowl

on the kitchen floor when I got downstairs. She'd missed her dinner and now she was missing her breakfast too and usually she lapped up all her food as soon as it was put down.

Brimalkin, Bazeeta, Amelka and Mystica wouldn't eat their food either. It was like they were refusing to eat because Pegatha wasn't there.

I felt soooo guilty. Why hadn't I checked my schoolbag? If I'd just done that then none of this would have happened.

Lilith said I had to go to school even though I didn't want to at all.

'You can't miss school,' she said.

'But Pegatha —'

'We've done everything we can to find her for the moment. Now all we can do is wait,' Lilith said. 'I'll let you know immediately if I hear anything.'

'Promise?' I said, because I didn't think I was going to be able to concentrate at school at all with Pegatha missing.

'I promise,' Lilith said. And I knew Lilith always kept the promises she made.

'I had a dream about you,' Angela said, as soon as I walked through the classroom door. 'You were flying on a broomstick past my bedroom window. How weird is that!'

Angela doesn't know I'm a witchling, of course. She just thinks I'm a perfectly normal girl who likes to wear black a lot. I tried to smile but I felt too sad.

'No luck finding Pegatha?' Angela said.

I shook my head.

Mrs Pearce came in then and Angela told her Pegatha was still missing. I thought Mrs Pearce might not care because I shouldn't have brought Pegatha to school in the first place, even though it was by accident. I thought Mrs Pearce might not even like cats very much because she was allergic to them and they made her sneeze. But

I was wrong. When Mrs Peace heard that I hadn't seen Pegatha since she'd run out of the classroom yesterday she was very concerned. Instead of working on our Egyptian project, Mrs Pearce got out a map of the local area and we made more posters to try and find Pegatha.

In the afternoon we even had an outing to the local park where someone said they thought they might have seen a tabby cat. But even though we looked all over the park we still didn't find her. Previously I hadn't always liked Mrs Pearce that much, but now I thought she was one of the best teachers in the world. And I was very grateful to everyone in my class for helping me too.

On the way home, I was still worrying about Pegatha. Lilith hadn't called and so it was unlikely there was any news. But then something very strange happened. Instead of going home my normal way, I turned down a street I'd never been down before. I don't why I did it. It was almost like I was being gently pulled along and then the pulling stopped and I stopped too.

I was standing outside a large old house with a sign that read:

BASTET'S
CATS' HOME

ALL CATS
WELCOME

Bastet was the other name for the Ancient Egyptian cat goddess Bast, the protector of cats, who I'd been learning about at school.

Cats peeped out of the windows and others played in the garden and lounged in the sun as I walked up the path and rang the doorbell. A few moments later, the door was opened by a smiling lady with green almond-shaped eyes.

'Hello,' she said. 'Can I help you?'

'I've lost my cat,' I told her.

'Have you? Oh you poor dear. Come on in,' the lady said.

Of course, I'd never normally go into a strange house,

but

somehow

my legs just

seemed to

walk me in,

and I wasn't

even

worried.

The lady's name was Amelia and she must have really liked rescuing cats because she had lots and lots of them from Abyssinians to Sphynx and Tonkinese and I thought she even looked a little bit like a cat herself. Some of Amelia's cats were sitting on the armchairs and sofa and some of them were lying on the bookshelves just like Mystica, Brimalkin, Bazeeta and Amelka often do at home. Everywhere I looked there were cats – white ones, grey ones, even tortoiseshell

ones! Two more were on the piano and three were on the windowsill looking out at passersby.

'How long has your cat been missing?' Amelia asked me.

'Since yesterday,' I said. 'I'm so worried about her.'

Amelia frowned. 'A cat did arrive here yesterday evening,' she said. 'I've been too busy to check the list of reported missing cats yet. She was very frightened and raced inside and hid under the sofa. She wouldn't come out until our oldest resident, a cat who was here even before I took over this place, managed to coax her out. She's a . . .'

'. . . tabby!' Amelia and I both said together.

Oh please let it

be Pegatha, I thought desperately.

'She might not be your cat,' Amelia warned me as she led me into her toasty warm kitchen.

I gasped as I looked down.

There, on a soft pillow in a basket curled up with an older black cat, and fast asleep, was Pegatha.

I longed to pick Pegatha up and hug her to me but I didn't want to wake her.

'I don't think she'll sleep for much longer now,' Amelia said, as we tiptoed back into the lounge.

She let me use her phone to call Lilith.

'I've found Pegatha,' I said. 'She's safe and well.' I told Lilith where I was and she said she'd be right round to collect us.

'I'm sure it's my fault Pegatha ran away,' I told Amelia while we waited for Lilith to arrive and Pegatha to wake up.

'Is it?' said Amelia.

I nodded and told her how Pegatha had been frightened when Mrs Pearce had started talking about a cat mummy.

'Nobody believes she can understand humans, but I'm sure she can. I think she might have thought we were going to turn her into a mummy . . .'

'The Ancient Egyptians loved their cats,' Amelia

said. 'They were the most revered of all animals.'

'I know,' I said. 'Did you know that Bastet was a cat goddess in Ancient Egypt? Did you call your cats' home after her?'

Amelia shook her head. 'It already had the name when I came here nearly a year ago,' she said.

'So how many cats have you got?' I asked Amelia. There seemed to be cats everywhere.

But she wasn't sure. 'They come and go as they please,' she said. 'Sometimes I have more, sometimes less but they are always welcome. I think cats know when they're welcome, don't you? Sometimes I don't know how I'm going to be able to afford to feed them all but I'd never turn a cat away.'

I looked out of the window as Lilith zoomed to a stop outside the cats' home in her bright red sports car, slammed the car door and came running up the path.

Her arrival must have woken Pegatha up because she came padding into the lounge, still half asleep. She gave a stretch like she always does and made the funny little noise that sounded very much like 'fish'. Then she stretched some more and looked round and saw me. She blinked as if she couldn't quite believe her eyes and then she ran to me and jumped into my arms.

'Oh Pegatha, I'm so pleased I found you,' I said, as I pressed my face against her soft fur. 'So, so pleased.'

It was time for us to go home, but just as we were about to leave, Pegatha jumped out of my arms and raced back to Moschi, the elderly black cat with a star on her forehead. She nuzzled into her, and the old cat licked Pegatha's head. It was

almost like Pegatha was saying thank you and goodbye. The old cat looked up at me and I was surprised to see she had turquoise eyes.

'Come on, Pegatha, let's get you home,' Lilith said.

'And then you can have some fish,' I said. 'Pegatha loves eating fish!' I told Amelia.

'So do all my cats,' she said.

Lilith started the engine and we were just about to drive off when Amelia came running out of her house, waving us to stop.

'Thank you! Thank you so much for all the lovely cat food in my kitchen. Fish–flavoured is their favourite!' she said.

I looked at Lilith. It was really kind of her to have magicked up some cat food for Amelia's cats, even though we are absolutely *definitely* not supposed to use magic outside Coven Road except in dire emergencies.

Lilith gave me a strange look back and then she turned to Amelia. 'You're most welcome,' she said.

Pegatha purred in my lap. 'You're the best cat in the world,' I told Pegatha. 'It doesn't matter if you're not a true witch's cat.'

Pegatha made a funny, sad little sound.

I kept quiet about Lilith breaking one of the laws of Coven Road because I thought it was so kind of her to give Amelia and her cats a present to say thank you for looking after Pegatha.

'Do you think Pegatha lived in Bastet's Cats' Home when she was little and that's why she went back there when she got scared?' I asked Lilith.

'Perhaps,' Lilith said, doubtfully.

I was sure I was right. I stroked Pegatha. I so wanted to be right.

'You came from the cats' home just like I came from the children's home, didn't you?'

Pegatha purred.

I looked over at Lilith. 'And then we both found a home together, with you.'

'And I'm very glad you did!' Lilith laughed.

On the way home we saw Sam putting a Missing Cat poster on a tree.

Lilith sounded the horn and then she stopped the car and pressed the button that made the roof open.

'We found her,' I called to Sam.

Sam came running over and gave Pegatha a stroke. 'I'm so pleased,' he said. 'No more running away again, Pegatha.'

Pegatha rubbed her face against his hand and miaowed as if she were agreeing with him.

'Isn't your new brother arriving today?' I asked Sam.

'Yes,' he said. 'I was keeping out of the way for as long as I could, but now I don't need to put up any more posters, I guess I'd better go home and meet him . . .'

Chapter 8

As soon as we walked in through the front door with Pegatha, the other cats jumped off the bookshelves and came running over to her. I'd never ever seen them all get off the bookshelves at the same time before!

To be honest Amelka, Mystica, Bazeeta and Brimalkin haven't always been the friendliest of cats to Pegatha. They never seem to want to play with her, but luckily she has me to play with. And they don't often play with each other anyway.

Now they were acting really strangely – twirling in and out and around her, miaowing and purring in greeting. Then they started to move even more quickly and the twirling got faster.

'What are they doing?' I asked Lilith.

'It looks like some sort of . . . cat dance,' Lilith said. She sounded just as surprised as I was.

'*Do* cats dance?' I asked her. 'I mean, properly?' I often pretended to get Pegatha to dance, but it wasn't serious.

Lilith smiled and shrugged. 'It certainly seems like they do. I think some of Coven Road's magic must rub off on the ordinary animals who live here – I've never seen them behave like this before!'

Amelka and Bazeeta intertwined with each other while Mystica and Brimalkin mirrored what they were doing. It really was very beautiful and went on for a minute or so before they surrounded me and Pegatha again – miaowing and purring and looking up at

Pegatha who I was still holding in my arms. Pegatha seemed to be just as happy to see them as they were to see her. She jumped out of my arms to join them. And then all five of them were doing the cat dance and Lilith and I were smiling and smiling.

I was so pleased Pegatha was back home with us and our family was complete once again. Pegatha, Brimalkin, Bazeeta, Mystica and Amelka twirled and swirled, swirled and twirled. And then Pegatha stood up on just her two back feet, like she does when I show her my feathery pen, and lifted one paw and then the other cats copied her.

And very soon after that Lilith and I just couldn't help ourselves, there was something about the cats' dance that was hypnotically irresistible. Now we were dancing and swirling and twirling too, laughing as the cats swirled and twirled and purred around us.

When the dance was over, Mystica, Amelka, Brimalkin and Bazeeta jumped back onto the bookshelves but this time they looked back at Pegatha and purred and miaowed and made a space for her on the bookshelves right in the middle of them all.

Pegatha looked up at me as if she were asking if it was OK for her to join them.

'Go on, then,' I said, bending down to give her a stroke.

Pegatha turned and jumped up onto the bookshelves and Lilith hugged me to her.

'Hungry?' she said, and I nodded.

I hadn't felt like eating much before with Pegatha missing, but now I realised I was very hungry.

'I'll get some food for Pegatha and the other cats too,' Lilith said. 'As it's a special occasion, I think they could have fresh fish for once.'

But when Lilith looked in the fridge she only had one small fish.

'Looks like it'll have to be cat food with a little fresh fish on top,' she said.

The phone rang and Lilith went to answer it. While she was gone I decided to try the duplicate spell on the fish and see if I could turn one fish into two. I dropped the blood leaf, cinnamon, gold candle and thistle water into the cauldron and chanted, '*Seeeorindggoi saheesta stowolhi staoorizlo.*'

Now there were two fishes on the plate.

I chanted the spell again – '*Seeeorindggoi*

saheesta stowolhi staoorizlo' — and two more fishes appeared. I did it one more time to make six fishes.

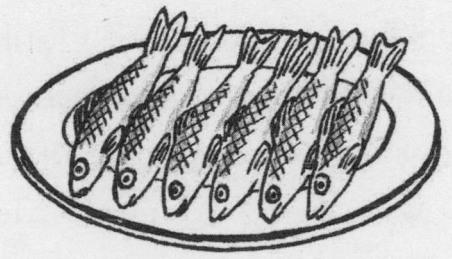

Lilith came back into the kitchen. 'That was Verity asking about Pegatha . . .' she started to say. Then she saw the fish. 'Oh my! Did you use the duplicate spell I taught you?'

I nodded, hoping I wasn't going to be in trouble for casting it by myself.

'I've never known it to work when only one witch has cast it before,' Lilith said, and then she smiled. 'But then I've never known a witchling as talented as you either.'

I'd forgotten it was meant to be done with two witches! I couldn't help feeling a little proud, but mainly I was just happy there was a fish for each cat – and even one spare! All the cats jumped off the bookshelf to eat their fish and then they all went back up there again. I was very pleased Mystica, Amelka, Brimalkin and Bazeeta were being so much friendlier to Pegatha now, although I secretly hoped she didn't stop sleeping on my bed at night.

I'd just finished eating when the phone rang again. Lilith picked it up and then turned to me.

'It's Sam and it sounds urgent,' she said.

I took the phone from her. 'Is everything all right?' I asked him.

'Yes, but you have to come over to the Woodland Wildlife Centre straightaway,' he said. 'There's someone you *have* to meet.'

I wanted to see his adopted sibling, but I also

didn't want to leave Pegatha because she'd only just come home.

'Ummm . . .'

'Pleeeaase,' Sam said. 'I wouldn't ask you if it wasn't really important and now that you've got Pegatha back . . . Please say you'll come.'

There was something different about his voice. It sounded more excited than sad.

'All right, I'll come,' I said. 'But I can't stay long.'

I got out my bike and pedalled over to the Woodland Wildlife Centre as fast as I could. The door was open and I gasped as I looked inside.

Sam had a yellow Labrador puppy snuggled in his arms.

'Oh Sam, he's lovely,' I said.

The puppy looked shyly up at me as I stroked him and then his tiny tongue licked my hand.

'As soon as Trevor and Tracey gave him to me, I knew you had to see him,' Sam said. 'I'm calling him Bobby.'

'Bobby's the latest member of our family,' Tracey said, coming in from feeding the chickens. 'And I think we can safely say that now our family's complete.'

She went into the kitchen to prepare some food for the deer.

Sam looked a bit embarrassed, until the puppy started licking him and then he started laughing instead. 'No – no – Bobby, stop it – it tickles!'

But the puppy was sure Sam didn't really want him to stop so he carried on.

'So it wasn't a new *human*,' I said.

'No,' Sam said, as Bobby stopped licking him and nibbled at his ear instead. 'Trevor and Tracey saw Bobby at the Dog Rescue Centre and thought he'd be the perfect companion for me. And he is.'

'Would you like a drink, Bella?' Trevor asked me.

I thanked him but said I had to be getting home. 'I'll be back to play with Bobby tomorrow, though.'

Sam grinned. It was so good to see him happy again too. I hoped he'd be as happy with Bobby as I am with Pegatha.

Chapter 9

'You won't believe who came to see Pegatha
while you were out,' Lilith said, when I got back.

'Who?' I asked her.

'Zorelda. She heard what had happened with
Pegatha and came straight round as soon as she

got back from the Witches' Convention.'

My heart started beating very fast. Zorelda's a bit scary. She isn't mean or tall or wide or even all that big but somehow wherever she goes, Zorelda seems to fill up the space just by being there.

'Pegatha jumped up into her lap and started purring as soon as she sat down on the sofa,' Lilith added. 'Zorelda's very good with animals and I'm sure she can communicate with them somehow. I've heard that some witches can but it takes years and years of practice.'

'Are you in very big trouble?' I said.

Lilith looked surprised. 'Me? No. Why would I be?'

'For breaking the Coven Road Rules by leading the broomstick search and magicking up cat food for Amelia's cats,' I said.

'Zorelda agreed it was an emergency and

didn't mind about the broomsticks. But I didn't
magic up any cat food,' Lilith said. 'I thought you
did that. I was going to say something to you –
but then it seemed mean when we'd just found
Pegatha.'

'No, I thought it was you.'

'You didn't perhaps do it by accident?' Lilith
asked gently.

I shook my head. I can usually tell now when
I use my magic. I hadn't even thought about
doing it, although it was a very good idea.

'How strange,' Lilith said.

And it was strange – very strange – but in a nice way.

'So what did Zorelda want then?' I said.

'First she wanted to see Pegatha alone. She called her the Little Wanderer and she asked me to leave the room. I went upstairs and had to stay there for so long I thought maybe Zorelda had left without saying goodbye. But she hadn't and finally she called me back down and said she was going to have a party to celebrate Pegatha's return and all the witches and their pets are invited.'

'That's brilliant!' I said. Witches' parties are just the best of the best and fortunately we have lots of them because witches love parties. I looked over at Brimalkin, Bazeeta, Mystica and Amelka sitting on the bookshelves. 'Can all our cats come?'

'Of course,' Lilith said. 'Zorelda said *all* the pets in Coven Road are invited.'

I'd never been to an animal witch party before and I was really looking forward to it.

'When's it going to be?'

'As soon as the sun sets,' said Lilith.

That's the good thing about witches and parties. You don't have to wait because witches can magic them up with a stir of their cauldrons and a snap of their fingers! It was a surprise having a party in the middle of the week, though – Zorelda must think Pegatha's return was very important. Which of course it was.

Pegatha jumped off the bookshelf and came to join me while I was getting ready for the party.

'You're one very lucky cat,' I told her. 'Everyone loves you and is glad you came home.' I tickled Pegatha in her favourite spot behind her ears and she purred with pleasure.

Pegatha's party was held in the communal gardens in the centre of Coven Road. Mr and Mrs Robson were already there with their dog, Waggy, when Lilith, Pegatha, Brimalkin, Bazeeta, Mystica, Amelka and I arrived. Waggy was very excited to see Pegatha and showed it in his usual way of wagging his tail like crazy. Then he gave Pegatha a lick on her ear but I don't think she liked that much because she batted at him with her paw and Waggy backed off. He still wagged his tail though.

'Good to see you home safe and well, Pegatha,' Redbeard said. He'd brought his

thirteen ginger cats with him to the party. Wherever he went, his cats followed him in a long line, like baby ducklings. They looked sweet and funny at the same time.

Verity looked very glamorous as always. She was wearing a black and lace velvet ballgown with long black gloves and she had twinkling jewels, which looked like diamonds, in her hair.

'Hello, Pegatha,' Verity said, bending towards her.

The tip of Pegatha's tail twitched as Verity's hand almost touched her. Then she miaowed and jumped onto Verity's twinkling head and up onto the flower rope that holds the magic swings that just swing by themselves without being attached to anything.

'I'm not a stepping stone!' Verity shouted after her.

I put my hand over my mouth so Verity wouldn't see I was laughing. Verity did see – but she laughed too.

At first, the animal party was much the same as our usual witches' parties: there were flying carpets and the magic buffet table where any food you can imagine magically appears. Tonight there was a second table with lots of different foods that pets liked as well. Amelka hopped up onto the table and came back with a sausage. Then Mystica tried it and came back with some

chicken and
Bazeeta came
back with a
fish-shaped
biscuit. But
Brimalkin
made me laugh
most of all
when he
hopped up onto

the table and the next moment started rubbing
some catnip against his face. Then he stopped
and went very still. Some music had started to
play.

'What's that music?' I asked Lilith, as soon as I
heard it.

It sounded very much like something we'd
listened to with Mrs Pearce for our Ancient
Egyptian project.

'The cat goddess had a festival called Bubastis where she used to play something called a sistrum,' I told Lilith.

'A sistrum?' she shouted, as the music got louder. 'What's that?'

I told her it was a special instrument they used in dances and ceremonies in Ancient Egypt. 'It's like an old sort of tambourine,' I shouted back, and as we listened we could hear the rhythm of

something that was sometimes soft and
sometimes loud but always jangling
rhythmically.

'Look!' Lilith said.

Pegatha was leading Mystica, Amelka, Bazeeta
and Brimalkin in the cat dance, standing on her
two back paws. Soon all the other cats from
Coven Road – and there were a lot of them –
joined in.

Other animals began to join in too. The unicorns were especially good!

Then we all gasped because it turned out Mr Robson was right! He'd said there was a dragon living in Coven Road – a very shy dragon who didn't like to be seen. No one else besides Mr Robson had ever seen it that I knew of, and I

didn't think it could have stayed hidden for so long. But the dance was too much even for the shy dragon to resist and he came to join in, along with the little blue penguins.

I'd never seen a snake or an alligator dance before but they obviously didn't want to be left out. The snake was very loose and wriggly and if

snakes could smile, I'm pretty sure that it would have been smiling. The hundreds of spiders on Mr Robson's coat all ran off it to do a spider dance on the ground. The butterflies that live on Mrs Robson's coat were already flying about but then they were joined by fireflies.

Finally it was too much for the rest of us to resist and all us witches of Coven Road were smiling and laughing as we twirled around each other and swirled and tapped our feet.

At midnight, Zorelda struck the golden witch's gong three times and everyone stopped dancing and turned towards the stage to hear what she had to say. Zorelda didn't seem to be speaking loudly but everyone could hear perfectly.

'A rare witch's cat has made herself known and graciously chosen to be the cat of one of the Coven Road witches,' Zorelda said.

Everyone was really excited and crowded

forward trying to get a glimpse of the true witch's cat, and no doubt hoping they were the one who had been chosen. Everyone that is, except me. I turned and walked the other way. I didn't want a true witch's cat. I had my Pegatha back – a perfectly ordinary tabby cat who was nevertheless the best cat in the world, to me.

'The witch's cat is probably for me,' I heard Verity saying loudly as I went past.

Her annoying remarks like that reminded me of why I didn't always like Verity and I didn't feel quite so guilty about being mean to her when Pegatha disappeared.

Pegatha might not be the least bit magical or rare, but I couldn't have loved her any more than I did even if she was the most magical cat in the world! She made me happy just by being herself, and that was enough.

But where was she? Now I came to think of

it, I hadn't seen her for quite a while.
'Have you seen Pegatha?' I asked
Lilith. But Lilith wasn't listening. She
was looking towards the stage where
Zorelda was standing, obviously trying to
see the true witch's cat too. She had a big
smile on her face.

I started to worry. Pegatha couldn't have
gone off again, could she? I could see
Mystica, Amelka, Brimalkin and Bazeeta
grouped together but no Pegatha.
I decided to go home and see if she was
there. But everyone was getting in my way
as they crowded forward trying to see the
true witch's cat.

'Excuse me . . . Please can I get past?
Excuse me . . .' I said, but no one moved
because Zorelda was still making her
announcement.

'And the lucky witch who has been chosen is none other than our newest witchling, Bella Donna.'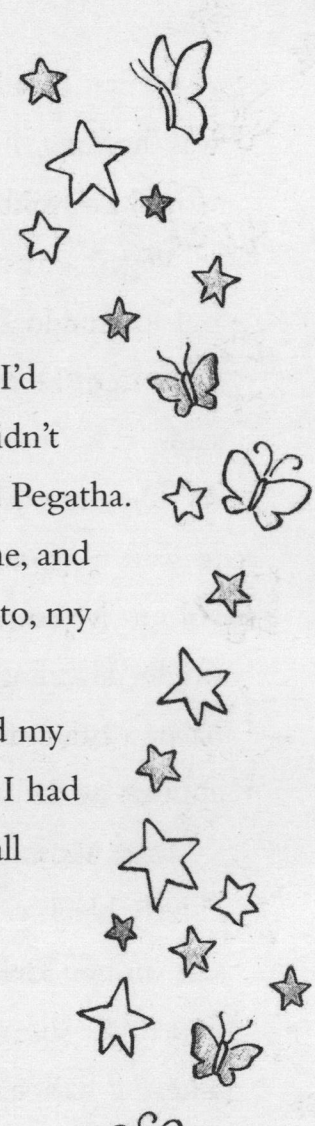

I gasped, but I carried on trying to go home, even though I'd heard what Zorelda had said. I didn't want a witch's cat. I only wanted Pegatha.

'Stop!' Zorelda commanded me, and even though I didn't want them to, my legs stopped moving.

'Come here!' Zorelda said, and my legs started walking forward and I had no choice but to go with them all the way up onto the stage as everyone stared at me and murmured. I was sure they were wondering why I didn't want a witch's cat.

At first I couldn't see the cat because Zorelda was holding her. But I could hear her and I would know that little purr anywhere.

'Pegatha?' I said. 'Pegatha!'

I looked at Zorelda who was holding my cat. 'I thought all true witch's cats had to be black,' I said.

'They usually are,' Zorelda said, as Lilith came to join us, 'but actually a witch's cat can be any colour it likes. It could change colour every single day if it wanted to. Older witches' cats have a star on their forehead that gradually appears as the years go by.'

'Like Moschi!' I said and I told her about the elderly black cat at Bastet's Cats' Home with the star on her forehead and the turquoise eyes. 'Do you think she was a true witch's cat too?' I said. Then I had a thought. 'Do you think it was Moschi who put the spell on Pegatha so we

couldn't see her when we looked in the crystal
ball? Was she trying to protect her?'

Pegatha made a funny little sound and
Zorelda looked down at her.

'Yes,' she said. 'Pegatha was very, very frightened when she arrived at the cats' home. She thought something terrible was going to happen to her. So Moschi put the spell on her. But then when Moschi saw how much Pegatha missed you she took off the hidden spell and cast a spell that drew you to Pegatha instead.'

So that's why I felt like I was being gently pulled down the street to the cats' home.

'But if Moschi's a witch's cat, why isn't she with a witch? Is Amelia a witch?'

Zorelda shook her head. 'No, she isn't. Witches can live for a very long time but not forever.'

'Oh. Moschi was very, very old,' I said.

Zorelda smiled. 'And is spending her well-deserved retirement with a woman who loves cats, in a warm kitchen on a soft pillow with plenty of food.'

I glanced over at Lilith. Did Zorelda know about the cat food magically appearing at the cats' home?

'I would say that Moschi is a very wise, very old witch's cat who has made her choice to look after other cats now,' Zorelda finished.

I took Pegatha from her and held her close to me. 'I always thought Pegatha was just an ordinary cat,' I said.

'So did we all,' said Zorelda, and Lilith nodded. 'I don't think even Pegatha knew she was a witch's cat at first. Instinct must have drawn her to Coven Road and to Lilith and you. Just like instinct drew her to the cats' home and Moschi.'

'But Pegatha isn't magical,' I said. Maybe she had to learn how.

Pegatha made that strange sound again – only this time it sounded almost exactly like 'Fish!'

And the next moment a huge pile of flapping fish appeared on the stage beside us. There were 'Oohs' and 'Aahs' and gasps from the watching witches.

Quick as a flash, Zorelda magicked up a pond for the flapping fish to be in. I'd love to be able to do magic in an instant, like that!

Pegatha gave a disappointed miaow, although she couldn't possibly have eaten all those fish.

Zorelda smiled. 'She will need help to learn to control her magic, just like you did. Are you willing to help her?'

'Yes,' I said, and all the witches clapped and cheered.

'So will Pegatha learn how to say more words?' I asked Lilith, after the party was over and we were all home. Mystica, Brimalkin, Amelka and Bazeeta were on their favourite bookshelves and Lilith and I were sitting on the sofa with Pegatha in my lap.

'Perhaps, or maybe she'll just have one word to say,' she said.

'Well, it is Pegatha's favourite word,' I said, laughing. If there was one thing I knew for sure, it was that Pegatha loved fish! 'Do you think Pegatha magicked up all that food for the other cats?' I asked.

But Lilith didn't know. 'If she did, it was probably by accident. As Zorelda says, she needs to learn to control her magic.'

I suddenly had a worrying thought. 'You don't mind that Pegatha wants to be my witch's cat, do you?' I asked Lilith. Pegatha was Lilith's cat before she was mine too, and if I were her, I might mind very much.

Lilith hugged me to her. 'I'd have been very happy if Pegatha had chosen to be my witch's cat. But you're my daughter, and so I'm even happier she's chosen you,' she said.

And I smiled because I knew that more than anything else Lilith cared about me. Lilith and I, Pegatha, Brimalkin, Mystica, Amelka and Bazeeta were all one big family, and always would be.

Have you read
all of
Bella Donna's
adventures?

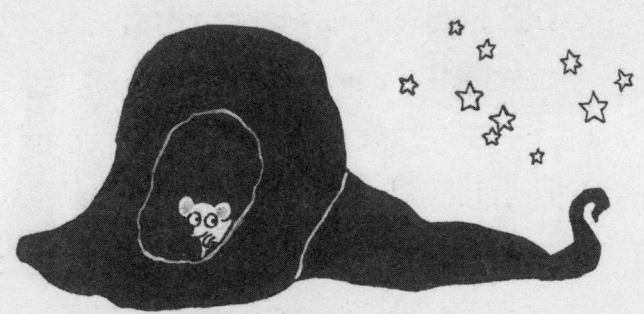

Bella Donna

Coven Road

Most girls dream of being a princess, but
Bella Donna has always longed to be a
witch. The only thing she wants more is
to find a family to take her out of the
children's home where she lives.
But no one seems quite right,
until she meets Lilith.

With Lilith's help, will Bella Donna
be able to make both of her
secret wishes come true?

Bella Donna

Too Many Spells

Bella Donna appears to be a regular girl at a
regular school with her regular friends,
but she has a secret – she is really
a young witch!

She's working hard at learning
her spells, and is desperate to
win the Spell-Casting Contest.
But when strange things start
happening at school, Bella begins
to wonder if she can really
control her magic . . .

Bella Donna

Witchling

Bella Donna is a witchling – a young witch who must keep her powers a secret, and only use magic when she's at home in the enchanted Coven Road.

But it's hard to stick to the rules when magic is such fun. There are so many things Bella can't quite resist, like flying on her broomstick and trying out some very special spells . . .

Bella Donna

Join Bella Donna online!

Explore and
download games,
puzzles,
activities,
and much more!

BellaDonnaOnline.co.uk